Brian James Freeman

Glen Chadbourne

This special signed edition of
Lost and Lonely
is limited to 1,000 copies.

Lost and Lonely

For Brad Saenz

With thanks to Kathryn, as always; to Robert Brouhard, Tabitha Brouhard, and Norman Prentiss for the technical support; to Simon Clark for the humbling introduction; and to Vincent Chong and Glenn Chadbourne for once again lending your amazing artwork to one of my collections.

Special thanks to Richard Chizmar for originally publishing several of these short stories and for telling me, "Be done with the story when you are ready." And to Brad Saenz for telling me, "It's not good enough." You were both right.

Table of Contents

Introduction

SIMON CLARK

THERE'S SOMETHING SO ELECTRIFYING about hearing dramatic news first hand. If your cousin stumbles into your house with scorched clothing, singed eyebrows and shouting, "You'll never believe what's just happened to me!" That's when everyone jumps to their feet and listens to every word he says.

I've given plenty of talks in the past and know that the audience's attention is bound to wander from time-to-time. That's when I pull out a sure-fire attention grabber. I'll suddenly go off topic, beginning with the words: "I remember the time I visited a maximum security jail. The audience I was addressing consisted of serial-killers." It never fails. People who are yawning, glancing at watches, or gazing dreamily out of the window, abruptly sit up straight, their surprised eyes lock onto me, and that's when I know I've got the audience back. I have their complete attention as I begin to describe my evening with notorious psychopaths. Meeting the serial-killers was a real event. Describing a first-hand experience as remarkable as that has an extra 'something' guaranteed to snare people's interest.

That's the knack of telling a good, attention-grabbing story, whether it's fact or fiction: what you say or what you write must have the power to hold your listener or reader. It must hook them and immerse them in the world you've created. The mark of a good story, in fact, makes us forget what's happening in the street outside, or the next room—and if it's really, really good it makes us forget ourselves for a while.

So, when I read Brian James Freeman's stories in this collection I had exactly that experience. The opening lines of "Something to Be Said for the Waiting" spirited me away to a world where a man reveals in a confessional, intimate manner what is worrying him. The story, told in an understated, economical way hooked me, drew me in, captivated me, alarmed me, and had me reading faster and faster to discover what happened in the end. Brian James Freeman's other stories in this collection have exactly the same effect. He has the brilliant ability to make you care about the characters. They are believable. What befalls them is plausible. I found myself connecting with the characters in an emotional way. Even one of the shortest of the stories, "Loving Roger"—a little gem of a tale that delivers a big punch—moved me. The plight of a frightened, confused girl was so touching I wanted to reach into her world and say, "It's okay. I'll help make everything all right."

Brian James Freeman, a writer with heart as well as consummate ability, takes us on fascinating and often disturbing journeys from intriguing beginnings to conclusions that are shocking, horrific, or deeply poignant.

Of course, as you'll have gathered, I'm being careful to avoid giving away too much about the plots. I don't want to spoil your enjoyment. I will say, however, they are all crisply written, effortlessly moving the reader through the mysterious landscapes of the author's potent imagination. There are surprising revelations, moments of genuine emotion, incidents of gruesome horror and, quite often, surprising twists in the tail. Each story is deftly painted with vivid imagery, allowing us a crystal clear view of what happens.

What struck me, when I was reading the collection, was that these lean pieces could easily be adopted as blueprints for a compelling TV series that wouldn't just horrify the viewers, they'd move them, too, and leave them wanting more. After all, another vital element of a great story isn't just that grabber of a beginning, it's when the story ends, and yet it doesn't end straight away in the reader's mind: the plight of the characters and their fate continues to resonate inside of us. We wonder what happens next.

What happens next right here is that as I draw this introduction to a close I invite you to continue reading, and enter the haunting places that Brian James Freeman has created—you're about to embark on a journey in the company of characters who will discover that their lives can become nightmarish in the blink of an eye.

Doncaster, England

January, 2016

Losing Everything Defines You

(Recording begins.)

If you're listening to this, I must be dead.

I have to wonder: who are you and how did you discover this tape?

Are you my agent's assistant searching for one last usable scrap of manuscript to sell?

That fifteen percent is tempting enough that he'd fly you down here to dig up whatever you could, isn't it? And depending on how the media covers my death, my work might be more popular than ever by the time you hear this recording.

Or are you a police detective trying to explain what happened to me? Maybe you don't think I had a heart attack, like the coroner will probably report. Or maybe my death will be far more gruesome than I can imagine and you're hunting for the sicko who killed me.

Or are you simply someone who wants an answer to the question so many people have been asking these past few months:

Did I kill my wife and son?

I've never been arrested, never been charged, but I've certainly been questioned.

The accusations have been made both publicly and privately, even as everyone has admitted I had no reason to hurt my family.

It's been three months since Wendy and Andrew vanished after an afternoon spent with friends at Black Rock Lake.

The police have no real suspects. My wife and son disappeared without a trace.

Well, unless you consider leaving our car where they left it to be a trace.

That and the blood.

Did I kill my wife and son?

Every morning, those words ring in my ears.

Every night, those words echo in my mind.

The answer?

I don't know.

I wish I could explain what happened.

Maybe then sleep would come a little easier at night.

Maybe I wouldn't hear the noises in the hallway outside my bedroom.

The slow, deliberate footsteps hitting every creaky floorboard like some Halloween-horror soundtrack.

Each night I cower in bed, the covers pulled up to my neck, the darkness wrapped around me like the grip of a dead lover.

I stare at the ceiling and I listen to the rumblings in the hallway.

There's no one else residing within this house, not anymore.

But I know what I'm hearing each and every night: my wife and son are coming home to me.

These sounds are driving me mad…yet I've learned waiting can be easier than knowing the truth.

These days I'm waiting to face my worst fear, which is better than actually confronting myself about what might have happened.

The whispering voices continue to ask:

Did you kill your wife and son?

It's a hard question to answer.

After all, they might not be dead.

No bodies were ever found.

(A click on the recording indicates the tape has been stopped and then started again.)

I miss Wendy and Andrew. I miss them terribly. At night, I wonder how I can continue on without my family.

People ask: *If everything was okay, why didn't you go to the lake with them that day?*

They ask this question when I say Wendy and I couldn't have been happier, when I say life was like a fairy tale.

We had a beautiful child, my books were selling well enough to pay our bills, and Wendy was preparing to quit her job at Happy Homes Realty to manage my business affairs full-time.

People ask this question even though our friends, the ones Wendy and Andrew spent the day with, repeatedly insist she didn't mention anything that would indicate we were having problems.

That day, when our friends asked where I was, Wendy told them the same thing I tell people now.

I was deep into writing a new book and I didn't want to lose the story, so I stayed home to work.

People believe that.

It certainly sounds like a good reason for a writer to skip a day at the lake with his beloved family.

Most days I *am* so drawn into my work that I can't escape the gravitational pull of the words. The world I'm creating becomes my reality.

But in this case, that answer isn't completely true.

Life wasn't as perfect as Wendy and I wanted people to believe. We lied to everyone, but not to ourselves.

Our personal divide started slowly, years ago, with me writing later and later into the night, pulling myself out of the real world until I wasn't even aware of my surroundings.

My son was growing up fast and I was missing all the important moments in his life but I couldn't help myself.

My work consumed me.

My imagination took me places my body never could.

Lost and Lonely

The need to transcribe those stories on paper was bordering on the compulsive nature of an addict.

In the months before Wendy and Andrew vanished, I barely spent any time with either of them.

I was too busy here in my office, hunched over my computer or talking into this tape recorder.

But please don't misunderstand me.

Even though a passionate fire no longer burned in my heart for my wife, it wasn't like I wanted to be with anyone else.

Wendy and I never discussed ending our marriage.

We talked to no one about the situation and we did the best we could with what we had.

I loved my wife and my son, even if I was becoming a stranger in my own house, and I would have done anything for them.

Yet if I told anyone these things, the accusations would get worse. You understand that, right?

21

The police have already questioned me as many times as you would expect given the circumstances.

The husband is always the number one suspect, but this is a small town where everyone knows everyone.

I am well liked and I had no motive.

My wife was well liked, too.

No one could have imagined things ending badly between us, but no one has an imagination quite like mine.

I've imagined a lot of things in my lifetime, and I understand the intensity of the bright spotlight I'm standing under.

After I called the police the day my family vanished, the men in blue searched the area and I was questioned about where I had been, what I was doing, and when I last heard from my wife.

The FBI arrived early the next day and soon after the media descended like vultures, attracted by the Amber Alert.

Within hours I was standing on the steps of the Sheriff's Office before the cameras, begging for help, pleading for the person who had my wife and son to let them go, since they had to have been kidnapped, right?

I repeated the special phone number the FBI had arranged so the kidnapper could contact us.

No one ever called.

(Another click on the recording indicating the tape has been stopped and started again.)

Can you hear the storm?

I don't know if this tape recorder is powerful enough for you to hear those sounds, but it's raining outside and the rainfall tapping at the window is steady.

The sound gets inside my head.

I wonder if I'm losing my mind.

Maybe I already did.

But here's what I've told anyone who will listen:

That morning, Wendy and I had breakfast and then she and Andrew departed for a day at the lake with our friends.

I headed upstairs to my office on the second floor of our home.

From ten in the morning until I awoke from an unplanned nap in the hour before sunset, I was lost in another world writing my new novel.

But when my wife and son didn't return from their afternoon at the lake, I went looking for them.

We live in a secluded house in the woods and our front door is nearly a mile from Rural Route #324, the main road to town.

My search didn't take long.

Wendy's white BMW was sitting at the end of our gravel driveway, parked like she had stopped to check the mailbox on her way home.

The driver's side door was open.

The right turn signal was blinking.

Lost and Lonely

That yellow light, flashing on and off, again and again, was hypnotic through the gloom of nightfall and spring fog.

The dome light inside the car glowed like the moon.

My wife and son were nowhere to be seen, but there was blood on Andrew's baseball glove in the back seat.

Just a little. A couple of nickel sized spots, really.

One of Andrew's flip-flops lay torn and tattered on the gravel nearby. Just one.

But there was no other sign of my family.

I yelled their names.

No one answered.

Panic consumed me.

I had forgotten my cell phone and the nearest neighbor was miles away.

I rushed back to the house and called 911 from the kitchen, wasting no time in the process.

Less than ten minutes later, the sheriff arrived and the questioning began.

(Thunder is audible in the background. The recording stops and starts again.)

Hold on.

There was another creaking floorboard in the hall.

Can you hear it?

I don't want you thinking I'm crazy. I'm not.

Everywhere I look, the world is closing in on me.

Maybe death would be better than my life, than living this haunted existence.

Do you really want to know why I'm recording this?

The *real* reason I feel compelled to spill my guts?

I'll tell you why.

The footsteps in the hallway are closer than they've ever been and I don't think the lock on the door will be of any use.

Maybe if I tell you everything I know, I can cleanse my soul.

So is it possible I killed my wife and son?

Yes, of course.

You just have to use your imagination a little bit and anything becomes possible.

(Another click. When the sound returns, the storm is considerably louder.)

Here's the truth about that day three months ago:

I really *was* caught up in writing a new novel, but there was another reason I stayed home and it's a good thing no one knows.

Wendy and I had a fight that morning. The cause of the disagreement isn't important. It really isn't.

But we *were* fighting and I'm sure you can understand why I haven't told anyone.

Instead of going to the lake, I stayed home and I wrote.

What I was writing will make me sound even guiltier, but I must be honest, at least now, at least on this tape for you, whoever you are, if there's even a chance this declaration will protect me from what I fear will happen soon.

My new novel was called *Losing Everything* and it was the story of a man who decides to kill his wife and son. He doesn't love his family and he needs the insurance payout. He plans and he plots, trying to determine the best way to get rid of them, and it finally occurs to him that people wreck their cars all the time. What could be less suspicious? So he disables the brakes on his wife's Camry.

But that's not a *confession*. Can you see the differences here? The differences are *huge*.

I loved my wife and son. Even if my love for Wendy wasn't the same kind of love it had been once upon a time, I still cared about her.

And my son? Andrew meant the world to me.

The insurance? I didn't need the money and I haven't gotten any, either.

Lost and Lonely

Wendy and Andrew are missing persons.

They weren't killed in a freak auto accident like the mother and son in *Losing Everything*. They disappeared at the end of our driveway.

But no one can ever know about *Losing Everything*, which is why I deleted all of my files from my computer and the cloud, and I burned the only paper copy of the manuscript in the fireplace.

No one would understand that the things I write about aren't based on my real feelings or real events.

If someone discovered *Losing Everything*, there would be even more questions and accusations, and I would prefer to do without both.

That's the last thing I need.

I'm having enough trouble staying sane as it is.

After being asked certain questions a million times, you find yourself questioning your own answers.

Some people asked why the police aren't tearing up the woods around my house searching for the bodies.

But the police *did* search the woods.

They searched for three days using cadaver dogs without finding anything.

No bodies, no fresh graves, no footprints, no nothing.

I might have been neglectful of my family's needs, I might have spent every waking hour alone in my office, but I *never* would have done anything to hurt my wife and son.

At least…at least I don't think I could have.

(Another click.)

Can you hear that?

The storm is getting worse. The wind is whipping around the house, the rain is smacking at the wooden siding, and the slow creaking in the hallway continues.

Two heavy footsteps.

Two lighter footsteps.

Can you hear that?

They're getting close, I think.

It's so cold in here.

Thunder just crashed outside the window, shaking the entire house like a bomb exploded.

Did you hear it?

I'll lose the lights soon, I just know it.

(Another click.)

There's one more truth I've kept hidden, denying it even to myself most days, but this might be my last chance to clear my conscience.

I've told you the day had turned to dusk, on the verge of night, when I awoke in my office, right?

But what I didn't tell you was this: I awoke to a whispering in my ear.

You understand why I've told no one about this, right?

Why I've even denied it to myself at times?

People would say: *If he hears voices in his head, who knows what he might have done to his wife and son!*

That's what they'd say and you damn well know it.

But the voice was very real.

The voice whispered: *if you hurry, you can save them.*

I jumped to my feet and ran from the room as if maybe the words had come from God himself, not even fully awake and not knowing why I was running but understanding there wasn't a second to waste.

I took the stairs two at a time, tripping at the landing and slamming into the wall, knocking the framed print of "Cutting the Stone" by Hieronymus Bosch to the floor where the glass broke.

A red handprint greeted me when I pulled away from the wall.

There was blood on my hands.

I was surprised by the cry rumbling from my throat as I stumbled through the foyer and into the living room, wiping my hands on my shirt as I moved.

The sounds my voice box was making were foreign to me. A wild animal caught in a trap might squeal like that.

My hiking boots by the living room couch were caked in mud. The mud was fresh.

The voice in my head screamed: *you have to go now!*

I didn't think, I just ran to the garage and jumped in my Jeep, starting the engine with a trembling hand.

Time was moving all wrong like I was stuck in slow motion.

I floored the gas and shot out of the garage into a strange night fog that had descended upon the woods.

The gravel driveway crunched under the Jeep's tires and the engine roared and I drove much too fast with my limited visibility.

The woods blurred past like something I might have dreamed the couple of times I experimented with drugs in college.

I spotted the car's yellow turn signal blinking through the fog in the distance.

The glow of the headlights.

The open driver's side door.

The tattered flip-flop.

The spots of blood on the baseball glove.

I screamed my wife and son's names into the night; I screamed until my lungs burned.

My heart sank.

I thought of the mud and the blood back at the house and I realized what I had to do.

My imagination is very vivid, but you don't need to be a natural born storyteller to understand how the police would connect the dots upon their arrival.

Leaving that mess would result in a trip to death row at Black Rock State Prison for sure.

I sped back to the house, leaving my wife's car exactly as I had found it.

Cleaning up the blood, the mud, the broken art print, and disposing of my shirt took less than thirty minutes, and then I called the police.

I called as soon as I could and…

Oh, God.

Are you still listening to me?

The power has died and the room is pitch-black except for the lightning, which sends splinters of light across the room.

That light splashes my shadow onto the wall like an accusation.

I hear someone outside the door.

My heart is pounding.

Can you hear my heart?

I can!

I can!

Throbbing inside my head like a bass drum!

The doorknob is slowly twisting.

The damn lock didn't do anything!

I can't look, but I know what'll happen next…

The door will swing open and Andrew's small voice will whisper something through his throat filled with mud and water and bugs, something about the ghastly realm that is his life after death.

Another creak!

Here they come!

Oh God!

The voice!

The door!

Oh God!

(The recording does not stop, but there is thirty-three seconds of storm sounds and nothing else. Then:)

"Daddy, why are you hiding in the dark? Mommy and me really miss you."

(end recording)

Loving Roger

EVERYONE MAKES MISTAKES, A TRUTH Patty knew all too well, which was why she believed in the power of forgiving and forgetting. Her mamma always said forgiveness was love and love was forgiveness. In the end, Patty knew mamma was right. No matter what mistakes Roger had made, Patty could never stop loving her husband.

The city noise pounded against Patty's temples as she slowed the rental car to a stop at one of the many busy intersections between her and the suburbs. The summer day would have been beautiful if she had been anywhere else in the world. A tractor-trailer roared past, horn blaring, engine snarling, black puffs of smoke spitting out of the chrome pipes behind the cab as the driver ran the red light.

Patty couldn't wait to escape the city. She had felt trapped in the rundown motel where she had been collecting her thoughts, and she would never go back there again. That place was loud and dirty and everyone was rude. The walls were made of cinderblock and the neighbors were so dangerous that all of the windows had metal bars on them.

"Everything will be better," Patty said, focusing on her goals. "I've learned from our mistakes."

She reached for the bottle of cheap champagne on the passenger seat, just to make sure it hadn't shifted. She worried about having the alcohol in the car. She wasn't even sure if that was legal and the new Patty who was driving home again almost didn't care. She and Roger had never imbibed, and she had begun to believe that was a mistake on her part. They needed to loosen up a little.

After confirming the champagne was okay, Patty removed a compact from her brand new purse. The price sticker and bar code were still affixed to the bottom of the peach-colored plastic shell. Her dress was also brand new, as were the lacy red bra and panties and the high-heeled shoes. She had never worn anything like this before. She wondered what her mamma would say and then she pushed the thought away.

Patty flipped the compact open and checked her makeup, lipstick, and hair in the tiny mirror. She felt so much older these days. Lines had formed under her eyes. Their fight had aged her badly, but she thought the makeup hid most of the damage.

Yes, there had been some problems lately, but those problems weren't *all* Roger's fault. Patty was seeing the world differently now. While in the rundown motel, she had found herself with a lot of free time to *really* contemplate what she wanted out of life, and what she had decided she wanted was to fix their mistakes and move forward. She hoped Roger felt the same way. They had to work together if they wanted to get back on the right track.

"Tonight, we'll make up for lost time," Patty said.

The light changed and someone behind her honked.

Patty raised her middle finger to the other driver—another thing she had never done before—and then she headed home, not looking back.

§

An hour later, Patty slowed to a stop in front of the two-story house deep in the heart of the suburbs. The street was tree-lined and the sidewalks were decorated with children's chalk drawings. Lush lawns dotted with trimmed shrubs and beautiful gardens surrounded the well-maintained homes. Everything was more colorful today than Patty ever remembered it being. More beautiful. More alive.

She realized she really *was* seeing life differently. She checked her watch and smiled. Roger wouldn't leave work for at least an hour. The champagne bottle would be chilled by then, and she would be ready to start their relationship anew.

She stepped onto the lawn. The grass was green and soft. A newfound love for her home and her yard and her neighborhood washed over Patty. Her heart fluttered and her skin quivered with unexpected warmth. She never wanted to leave again.

Patty approached the front door and shifted the bottle of champagne under her arm. As she reached for the doorknob, she stopped dead in her tracks.

She had forgotten her house key.

Panic rose inside of Patty and her breathing became clipped. Her hands trembled. She was so close to making things right again and then something like this had to happen. How could she have been so stupid? Her plan was ruined!

"No," Patty whispered. "*No,* I can do this."

She sucked in two deep breaths and then made her way around to the back of the house, pushing through the flowering bushes that enclosed the brick patio. She crossed the patio and stopped at the sliding glass door. She said a little prayer, reached for the handle, and pushed. The door slid open with a squeal.

Patty smiled brightly and stepped into the kitchen, the bottle of champagne gripped tightly in her hand. The yellow patterned linoleum floor was spotless and the ceiling fan spun in lazy circles. Cool air washed over her sweaty skin.

Something was different, though. On the counter was a wooden knife block holding seven specialty knives. Patty had always wanted a set like that, had pointed them out to Roger a million times at Monkey Ward, but he always claimed they were too expensive. Then she noticed an even more dramatic change: the new Kenmore refrigerator. She hardly believed her eyes. She had wanted a new refrigerator since they first moved into the house so many years ago and Roger always said they couldn't afford one.

Excitement rose inside of Patty and her heartbeat quickened. Had Roger come to the same realization she had during their separation? Was he making an effort to win her back, too? What else might he have planned? Her mind spun at the possibilities.

Yet, something wasn't right and her heart understood that before her brain. A frown formed on Patty's tired face.

There were comic strips and newspaper clippings and "honey do" lists held to the refrigerator by a variety of magnets. Some of the magnets were shaped like animals, others like clouds, and still others like fruits and vegetables.

None of these magnets or the collected pieces of paper belonged to Patty.

"Who are you?" a woman asked from the dining room. "What are you doing?"

Patty spun around and the champagne bottle slammed into the edge of the kitchen counter. Patty and the other woman both jumped in surprise as the bottle shattered. The liquid inside sprayed into the air as shards of glass skipped across the floor on a wave of foamy liquid.

A moment passed and neither woman moved. Then their eyes rose from the wet mess and locked on each other.

"Who are you?" the woman asked again. She laughed nervously. She was much younger than Patty, with blonde hair and blue eyes and trim legs. The woman reminded Patty of the girls she had known in her college days, back when she first met Roger at a mixer. Patty had seen how Roger looked at those girls.

"*Who* are *you*?" Patty asked. A knot twisted in her stomach.

"My name is Sally." The woman's voice was a little less harsh this time, showing a hint of concern. "Are you okay, hon? What are you doing here?"

"I live here with Roger. What are *you* doing here?"

"I'm sorry. You must be confused," the woman said. "This is my house."

Patty finally realized who this woman was, who this woman had to be. The whore. This was the goddamned whore who had seduced her husband!

The rage Patty had been suppressing for a lifetime boiled over. Waves of heat flowed through her body and her hands trembled from the surge of adrenaline. A lot of people had taken advantage of Patty over the years, but she had never been so consumed by anger when faced with their betrayals.

Patty's vision flashed red as she reached for the wooden block on the counter and selected the largest knife. When she turned back toward the dining room, she saw the shock on the whore's face.

Patty took a step, kicking the base of the broken champagne bottle across the foamy kitchen floor.

"No, wait a minute," the woman said as she backed away, raising her hands. "What are you doing?"

As Patty moved, she remembered the events of a day much like this one many years ago when she had come home early from work.

She had discovered Roger and that woman from across the street doing terrible things like animals in heat. God, the awful sounds they had made!

Patty's anger and confusion merged with the memory of the endless river of blood splattering everywhere. Patty was home again and she saw every little detail and she had to do *something* to make them stop.

The woman named Sally, now backed into a corner, said: "Please don't hurt me! Please listen!"

But Patty couldn't listen. She had to make Roger and the awful woman stop what they were doing. She had to help Roger understand the mistake he was making.

She loved him so goddamned much. Why couldn't he understand that?

Patty raised the knife and prepared to show her husband exactly how much she loved him, and she would keep showing him until he understood that her love was endless and eternal.

She would love Roger again and again, and she would never, ever stop.

How the Wind Lies

DURING THE YEARS HIS FAMILY LIVED IN the colonies, William Carver was firm but fair so long as his wife and children remembered his rules for good living: calloused hands do the work of God, defend thy honor only at the expense of thy humble heart, delay no task lest the load grow even heavier, and never speak a lie lest thy lie becometh the truth.

Yet life in the colonies felt like someone else's memories as William worked under the blazing sun on the flowered plains, tilling the land beyond their vegetable garden for additional planting to prepare a stockpile for the winter. The change in seasons was still months away, but the previous winter had nearly claimed their lives and he would take nothing for granted.

William turned the soil by hand with the hoe his father had made in the old country. That was fine. Difficult labor in the heat of the summer sun left him sweating and aching, a reminder that God rewarded His hardest workers. William was a bear of a man and he attacked his tasks with an almost religious fervor.

On a clear day, he could see for miles across the flatlands, and the grasses surrounding the homestead often danced and swayed in the gentle breeze. Since his family's arrival here, William had discovered the winds of these western plains spoke in a variety of voices, many he had never heard in the colonies. Sometimes the wind was enraged, pushing black clouds across the endless sky. Sometimes the wind whispered and soothed, cooling the sweat on his neck.

With the exception of the Indians, who had left them alone so far but could sometimes be heard in the distance, William felt like his family was living in total isolation. That certainly hadn't been the plan when they departed the town they had always called home, but at least they had escaped the danger back east. He thanked God for that every morning and every night.

There were three other homesteads nearby, abandoned and overgrown. William did not dwell on the dilapidated nature of the cabins he had once helped build. There was no time to memorialize the people who had lived within the homes for such a short time. Instead he focused on the future, for he only had so much energy to give each day and this land demanded everything from him.

William returned his full attention to his work. His eldest son George should have been with him, but Sarah had suggested the boy could use a day to play and explore, and William had eventually decided she was correct, as he so often did. His wife was wise and he took her counsel seriously.

Now, though, George came to his father from the fields to the west and said, "Something's killing the buffaloes."

William studied his boy. Young George Carver was thirteen and full of bluster and noise, but he had never told a lie as far as his father knew.

Sarah worked quietly out of earshot, scrubbing clothes in a wooden tub filled with water from the nearby stream. The young twins, Peter and John, played in the dirt by the cabin's door and they took no interest in the conversation.

"What do you mean?" William asked.

"Their fur is white and their eyes are milky and the stench is awful." George removed a handful of white fur from the pocket of the pants his mother had sewn for him. The tufts floated away on the breeze.

"Go to the creek and wash your hands, boy," William said. "I'll see to this."

"Yes, sir."

William walked into the fields of waving grasses that continued for miles in every direction.

He walked with a heavy heart.

He feared he knew what was killing the buffaloes.

§

William studied the horizon for any sign of the terrifying Indian tribes they had been warned about when they headed west. He rarely had time to reflect upon matters beyond the immediate needs of his wife and children, but as he ventured further from the homestead, he considered how they had come to live in this place. If what he feared was true, the journey had not put enough distance between them and the danger.

Ten families had set out across the country, fleeing the terror ravishing their community, but only four families reached the open plains. Some turned back when supplies ran low and some were claimed by the big river, drowning when the rapids flipped their rafts while the other helpless travelers watched in horror.

The four families who survived built their homesteads just in time for the first brutal winter, but that wasn't enough to protect them. Their numbers dwindled as the snowy days marched on, and by the time the warmth of spring awakened the land, the Carvers were the only ones left.

William had done his Christian duty and given those other men, women, and children a proper burial as they passed. Treat thy neighbor as you would treat thy kin, he always said, yet their names were already fading from his mind. They were with God and memories of those who had passed served no meaningful purpose to his daily tasks.

William was the only man left, and as such he carried a tremendous weight upon his shoulders. He rarely slept, spending his nights watching for Indians and other threats that might lurk beyond the safety of their homestead.

He was also waiting for something he didn't dare speak of.

There was a very specific sound, one he had only heard once before, back in the colonies when he suffered a very close call that could have ended with his demise.

The sound was a harsh whistling, like the cry of an animal stabbed by a hunter's knife, and yet it was both loud and soft as it rose and fell, beckoned and repelled.

If William heard that sound again, their journey had been for nothing and his entire family would almost certainly perish.

🌀

William found the dead buffaloes easily enough. Their death scent was carried to him by the wind. The odor was unmistakable. The buffaloes reeked as if they had been corpses for weeks, not the mere hours every other indication pointed toward. There were tacky drops of blood on the grass and the last terrified bowel movements hadn't solidified.

"My Lord," William whispered, covering his mouth with his hand.

He approached the nearest buffalo with trepidation, pulling back the bleached fur from the top of the head. He did not relish the thought of touching the animal, but he had to be certain his instincts were correct.

In a shredded patch of fur, he discovered what he had feared: two puncture wounds of equal size through which the buffalo had been drained completely of blood.

William did not linger at the massacre. He sprinted back through the tall grasses as the smell of death chased him on the wind.

In the distance, Sarah screamed and William ran even harder.

§

The screaming ceased before William reached the homestead, his heart pounding hard in his chest.

George and Peter were sobbing as they held onto their mother in the clearing by their cabin. Sarah cradled little John in her arms, rocking him as she had when he was a mere baby. He was dead, his skin as pale as chalk, his eyes milky white.

For William, the cause of death was unmistakable. There could be no other answer. Rage and revulsion and despair flooded through him. He dropped to his knees and grabbed the boy away from his wife. John's head rolled loosely on his tiny neck.

"Where was he?" William demanded.

"He and Peter were behind the other cabins," Sarah said through her tears. "I went for them to begin their chores and I came upon John in this state. I screamed and screamed."

William turned toward Peter. "Son, what did you see?"

"Nothing, father," Peter said, tears pouring off his face like sweat. "He just fell dead in the grass."

"Did you see him fall?"

"No, I was watching the clouds."

"All of you, get inside."

His family didn't question his command. They hurried into the cabin and closed the door, leaving William with his dead son.

After fortifying his courage, William lifted John into his massive arms and hugged him like a ragdoll. The boy seemed to weigh nothing and was far too light for a corpse, which normally grew heavier in death.

William closed his eyes and ran his hand through John's thick hair, which was dry and brittle like aged straw. With a grimace, he used his fingernail to explore deep into his son's scalp. He discovered a wet mess encircling two wounds in the skull, just as he had expected and feared.

John was drained of blood.

§

William dug a grave for his son alongside the other crosses marking the resting places of their travel companions. His enormous hands ached from the digging, but the pain reminded him that he was a man with responsibilities to honor.

The stink emanating from the corpse was horrendous, another sign the boy had been killed by the beast they had hoped to escape. But how could that nightmare of a monster have known where to find them? It didn't seem possible, but William was not a man to deny the truth he witnessed with his own eyes. The beast was here and would need to be dealt with or their own lives would be taken from them.

William gently placed his son in the hole and spoke a short prayer. John's withered corpse lay small and helpless in the shallow grave.

William covered his boy with the freshly-turned soil.

Just as he had buried the others.

૭

That night, as William lay awake in the darkness and listened to his wife and children quietly sobbing, he contemplated the myth of the Salem Vampyre: how it sucked the blood directly from the brains and how the odor of the corpse would become unbearable.

The Salem Vampyre's reign of terror was the reason the ten families had headed west. No one could determine where the Vampyre was hiding and, unlike the Vampyres of the old country, this one didn't seem to mind the light of day. He could be anywhere. He could be anyone.

Not only did the townspeople fear becoming the Salem Vampyre's latest victim, but some said if even a drop of the Vampyre's blood touched your flesh, you would become his servant and stalk your loved ones and neighbors.

Rumors ran rampant that others were already joining the Vampyre in his hunts. Neighbors turned against each other and there were no safe quarters to be found. No one could be trusted.

There was talk, so much talk, but one particular thought returned to William again and again.

In the old country, you would push a stake fashioned from wood through the heart of the Vampyre, causing the beast to burst into flames and die.

William spent the night considering this. He did not sleep.

§

"Are you certain you didn't see anything?" William asked his wife the next day. They sat at the table where they had eaten all of their meals, many of them very meager, especially during that first winter. Sarah's eyes were stained red from the force of her weeping.

"I'm certain. John and Peter were playing and when I went outside to remind them of their chores, John was lying in the grass. I thought he was fooling me until... until I saw his pale skin."

"Where was George?"

"He had gone to the creek, as you instructed. Do you really believe the Salem Vampyre has come?"

"Yes. Somehow the monster tracked us, but I will stop him once and for all."

🌀

William crouched inside the cabin, using his hunting blade to sharpen one end of a slat he had taken from his dead son's bed. Slivers of wood piled between his feet like shed skin.

His mind and body were exhausted, but while he worked, William remembered how he had nearly met the Salem Vampyre face to face back in the colonies. He had been making his way home late one night after drinking ale, and he had taken the long way so he could watch the moonlight dance on the narrow river racing to the nearby ocean.

The world was very calm, as if William were the last man in the colonies, until a harsh whistling from the woods broke the peace. The sound was unlike anything he had ever heard before. The whistling rose and fell, like a song carried on an unnatural wind, and the noise chilled him to his bones. This was both a calling and warning spoken in the same foreign voice, summoning him while also trying to push him away. There was something terrible and haunting, yet also inviting and calming within the flurry of sounds that grew closer.

William couldn't help himself; he found his feet moving without thought. He was several steps into the woods when the whistling stopped as quickly as it had started. The spell was broken and William stumbled back toward the path, horrified by his loss of control. He hurried home, and by the time he reached his own bed, he was convinced the sound was merely a lingering effect of the drink he had imbibed.

The next day the patriarch of the Smithee family was found near that very spot on the path, dead, the latest victim of the Vampyre.

Had William investigated the noise, had his feet continued to push him forward, he might have joined Mr. Smithee in the hands of the Lord, leaving his poor family to fend without him. That had been a very close call indeed.

Not more than a week later, William and his family and the others had pooled their resources to purchase wagons and supplies. They headed west, where rumor had it you would be safe from the monster walking among them.

Yet here was William fashioning a stake from his dead son's bed while George and Peter played just outside the door, honoring his instructions not to wander. Off in the distance, Sarah washed in the creek. She was badly shaken by the sudden loss of their son after they had traveled so far to start this new life, and William had suggested a cool bath might calm her nerves.

He took great care as he carved the stake, knowing his calloused hands were doing the work of God, and he was nearly finished when Sarah screamed. The piercing wail was much closer than the creek. William bolted toward the door but stopped dead in his tracks once there, unable to believe what awaited him in the bright sunlight.

Peter lay on the ground not far from the cabin, pale and bloodless and as dead as his twin brother. Sarah had fallen to her knees beside the withered boy. George stood nearby, his face blank.

William scanned the area. They were alone. There was no one else to be seen for miles.

He stumbled out of the cabin on trembling legs and fell to his knees next to his wife. Together, they held their son.

George watched. His expressionless face did not change.

⑨

In the scorching light of the unforgiving sun, William dug another grave.

The blazing heat and the pain deep in his heart left him shaking, but he did not stop until his work was done.

ⓢ

"I'm scared," Sarah whispered that night, holding their last son as he slept. Her eyes were drifting closed. She was exhausted from the terror of the last few days, but she didn't dare release little George from her grip.

William checked outside again, gazing into the darkness. The grasses swayed in the wind, but there was no one to be seen. Or heard. They were alone and his mind was ablaze with thoughts that troubled him.

George must be our Salem Vampyre. He has to be. He was the only one around both times. And he is the one who found the dead buffalos. It has to be him. But Sarah doesn't know...

William slumped onto the wooden chair like a broken old man being crushed by the weight of the world. He watched his son sleeping in candle-light that flickered and sent shadows dancing across the room. Sarah held the boy tightly, as if she feared he might float away. Her eyes had closed.

A voice that sounded much like William's own whispered inside his head: *Kill him while you have the chance.*

No, I can't, William thought. *He's my boy.*

Who else must perish before you'll do what must be done? the voice asked. *Delay no task lest the load grow even heavier.*

The only sound in the cabin was the gentle calling of the wind sweeping across the plains, but George's eyes snapped open. The boy said nothing, but he turned his head toward his father. Their eyes locked. Staring at one another in the uneven glow of the candle, William spotted a glimmer in the boy's gaze. An unnatural light.

I must, William decided. *I must finish this before it's too late. He's not my son.*

Yes, the voice agreed. *Your work must be completed. It will be quick. Plunge the stake into his black heart and he shall burst into flames, ending the horror.*

William removed the stake from under the table where he had secured it with a bit of rope. He grabbed George from Sarah's arms with one rough tug and dragged the boy into the middle of the room.

Sarah's eyes opened and she looked around, confused and disoriented. She saw what was happening and she reached for her son, but she moved much too slowly in her dreamlike state.

"May the Lord forgive me," William whispered as he knelt over George and raised the stake above his head.

George's mouth opened and William drove the stake into his heart and cut off any words he might have been preparing to speak. His high-pitched squeal of agony tapered into rough coughs and he convulsed, spitting blood. William fell backwards in his haste to avoid the fluid, lest he risk catching whatever had infected his boy.

George shook and shuddered, his fingers clawing at the rough floor. Sarah crawled to her son and pulled him into her arms as blood poured from his mouth. The stake remained in his chest.

"Get away from him!" William demanded, but his wife either did not hear his order or she ignored him for the first time in their marriage.

"Mother," the boy whispered, his eyes locking on hers before he took one last, shuddering breath.

Moments passed, but George did not burst into flames as the Vampyre was rumored to do upon the arrival of his own death. Instead, Sarah held him and rocked him and cried his name.

"No," William whispered, pressing his hands against the sides of his head. "He didn't burn. It wasn't him."

Sarah stroked their dead son's hair as if she were in a trance. After a few minutes, she gently laid George on the floor and staggered to her feet.

She studied her husband as if he were a stranger whom she had never met before, a stranger with madness in his eyes.

"Why?" Her voice cracked and her hands trembled.

"I had to stop the Salem Vampyre," William said. "I thought it was the boy. It *had* to be him."

Sarah stood there, the candlelight flickering across her face. She seemed to be staring a great distance beyond the walls of the cabin. Her mouth opened and closed several times, as if she wanted to say something but had forgotten how to form the words.

When Sarah moved, she moved quickly, lunging across the room and swinging her fists at her husband. She landed blows with the fierceness of a woman who had been pushed to the brink of insanity.

She had never done anything like this before in her entire life, and William recovered from his surprise and began easily deflecting her punches. He saw the unnatural light burst to life within her eyes. It was the hunger of the monster that had stalked them from the east.

William shoved his wife away, sending her flying like a ragdoll.

"This madness must *not* continue," he said, bending over and pulling the stake from George's limp body.

Sarah scrambled into a sitting position against the cabin wall. She tried to stand, but William was too big and too fast. He grabbed her foot and dragged her next to their dead son in the middle of the room.

Sarah's eyes widened and she gasped as William raised the bloody stake and brought it down. He thought she might scream, but all of the breath flowed from her mouth in a wounded hissing noise. She winced and a trickle of blood escaped her lips. She blinked several times, slowly, and then the light glowing in her eyes was gone. She didn't move.

William backed away, waiting for his wife of so many years to burst into flames.

But she didn't burn either.

William stared at her body, unable to comprehend what this meant at first.

"Neither of them was the Vampyre? But there's no one left..."

The voice in his head replied: *You, William, you're the only one left. You killed your wife and sons.*

"I had to," William said.

You killed them. You killed them all.

"I had to stop the Vampyre!"

William... what Vampyre?

William flung the cabin's door open and walked out on legs that did not feel like his own. He fell to his knees below the watchful eye of the bright moon.

Memories collided, forming and breaking apart again and then snapping back together. He saw people screaming, men and women and children alike, their faces round and pale. He had tried to forget who they were, but how could he forget his closest friends and neighbors who had traveled to this place with him based on his promise that they would be safe from the terror?

In these memories, William saw their horror as they raised their arms to block a blow or avoid an attack, but they were overpowered, each and every one. They were struck down by someone much bigger and stronger, and their chests were pierced by a sharpened stick. Blood sprayed from the wounds. No one burned. No one ever burned.

Disgust rose inside William as he realized who had wielded that stake. His stomach clenched and dropped in his gut.

All of the memories poured back into his mind like a rain cloud bursting. He could remember the slick blood coating his face as he did what he thought he had to do, his own eyes wide and yet blinded by fear.

He had killed his friends and family in his hunt for the Vampyre. Yet, after each murder, his mind closed upon itself, blocking the memories and the truth. He told himself they had died of a sickness and he repeated this lie often enough that he truly believed it.

"What have I done?" he called into the night.

The voice whispered: *Never speak a lie lest thy lie becometh the truth, William.*

William crawled back through the open door and into the cabin. He continued across the floor to the bodies of his dead wife and son, dragging himself with bloody fingers.

He considered the terror of living on the plains all alone with the memory of what he had done. The endless view of nothing but the flowering grasses waving at him. The howl of the wind in the night as it shook the cabin. The bitter winter that at times seemed to be without end.

Defend thy honor only at the expense of thy humble heart, William.

He grabbed the stake, which was dripping with the blood of his wife and son. He aimed the point toward his own chest. It was time for his hands to truly do the work of God and put an end to the horror.

William whispered a prayer, but as he prepared to jerk the stake deep into his own chest, another voice whispered in the back of his mind.

This was the voice of Sarah, and hearing his dead wife speaking to him nearly stopped his heart.

She said: *William, my love, if there is no Vampyre, how do you explain the dead buffaloes drained of their blood? Or Peter and John?*

Sarah had always given him the wisest council, he realized, and tears formed in his eyes.

A noise outside the cabin seized William's attention, sending a shiver down his spine as if an icy hand caressed his back.

A whistling started deep in the grasses. The familiar sound rose and fell, growing shriller with each passing second, approaching the cabin. Closer and closer and closer still.

Just outside the doorway, the whistling stopped.

William stood, nearly collapsed, then steadied himself, the stake still gripped tightly and ready to be used.

He approached the door with heavy legs that fought his every movement. He didn't really want to learn what might or might not be waiting for him outside the cabin, but he also couldn't stop himself.

William opened the door.

He stood there for a moment, terrified beyond words.

Then William screamed, and his scream, like the screams of so many others, was carried away on the wind.

Perfect Little Snowflakes

EVEN IN THE DARK, THE MOTEL ROOM WAS ugly.

Melissa was just sixteen, had never spent a night away from home, and this was not where she wanted to be.

Matthew pushed past her and into the bathroom, closing and locking the door. Melissa stood in the doorway, the winter wind blowing around her, cutting through her dress, biting into her flesh as if she wore nothing at all.

They had left the Black Hills Diner in such a hurry, Matthew practically dragging her by the arm, that she had forgotten her jacket in the booth. She wondered if someone would put it in the Lost and Found box at the front of the restaurant. She loved that jacket.

The walls of the motel room had been painted beige years ago and the popcorn ceiling was yellowed. This was the sort of place that didn't have a "no smoking" policy until the legislators in Harrisburg declared that particular vice to be against the law, at least when it came to restaurants and hotels.

There was a frayed wicker chair, a twin bed with two pillows tucked under the green covers, and a battered wooden dresser with an ancient television and a faded placard:

Welcome to the Black Rock Motel! Checkout is Noon. Sorry no smoking! Enjoy your stay!

There was a scuffed nightstand with a wind-up alarm clock and a Gideon Bible. The hands of the clock pointed at eight sharp, but Melissa knew it was closer to eleven. Her parents would be wondering where she was.

Melissa closed the door, leaned against the wall, and rubbed her temples. A dull headache had been building all week. Her forehead throbbed. Her thin lips were chapped and they hurt.

She took two steps and sat on the edge of the bed, the box spring screeching under the weight of her petite frame. She picked up the alarm clock and wound the metal key, not bothering to set the correct time. The minute hand slipped forward with an audible click.

Melissa wrapped her arms around her belly. It was still small. For now.

She hadn't told anyone other than Matthew—not her parents, not their friends—but everyone would learn her secret eventually. She and Matthew had two more years of high school left and they couldn't exactly hide a baby.

Maybe in the rest of the world this situation was acceptable these days, the sort of thing that might even get you a television show, but not in the small town of Black Hills, a place where people lived for the talk. The gossip. The community would whisper about how Melissa loved spreading her legs, would spread her legs for anyone, in fact. Gossip was king. It didn't matter that Matthew had been her first. The first boy to say he loved her and the first boy she kissed and the first boy she truly loved. They had taken things so much slower than most of their peers. None of that mattered.

Melissa considered herself a modern, independent woman, even if she was still just a little girl in her father's eyes, but this week had tested her. She had never understood how circumstances could change so quickly and so unexpectedly without any hint of trouble on the horizon. One day she was a teenage girl in love with her boyfriend, the next day she was a mother-to-be with no idea what to do.

The bathroom door remained closed. She loved Matthew, but he wasn't handling this as well as she had hoped. He had barely said a word since she shared her news with him earlier tonight. He had mumbled something about dinner and he drove them to the Diner where he said nothing and then he had mumbled something about them needing to leave and they had left in a hurry and then he had mumbled something about her staying in the truck when he stopped at his father's house on the outskirts of town.

Matthew had returned a few minutes later with a wad of cash he had probably stolen from his father's drinking stash and then he drove them to this motel where she waited in the truck while he paid for a room.

Melissa stood again and opened the curtains, revealing the smudged window. Falling snow painted the night sky white. There was a rocking chair outside the door, rocking in the winter wind. The flickering neon signs proclaimed BLACK

ROCK MOTEL and VACANCY. It always said VACANCY these days.

Matthew's second-hand truck was the only vehicle in the parking lot. Beyond that was the road and beyond the road was the forest, thick with barren trees and dead underbrush. In the distance, deep in the valley, the lights along Main Street bisected the small town they called home.

Melissa wished everyone would just go away for a while so she could think. The world was a meaningless hum inside her head, a silent bombardment of the accusations and taunts she knew would be coming. She was weary, even with Matthew here. Maybe *because* Matthew was here. She had thought things would somehow get better once he knew the situation they were in, but she had been wrong.

"You okay?" she asked the locked bathroom door. Water splashed in the sink. No reply.

Melissa returned to the bed and she watched the falling snow and she thought about the growth inside her belly, the baby who couldn't be much bigger than a few clumped snowflakes.

When she was a little girl, her father had once drunkenly told her that all children were like perfect little snowflakes: each one was different and unique and flawless in conception, but you never knew where they would land once they hit the ground. She still didn't know what he had meant and, like most of his drunken sayings, he probably didn't either.

The bathroom door creaked open and Matthew emerged. His baggy pants hung around his hips. He had splashed water on his face and his hair was wet. There was a heaviness in the way he moved, as if he were the one who had been wrestling with a week of sleepless nights punctuated by nightmares and terror.

"How are you doing?" Melissa asked.

Matthew didn't reply. He sat in the wicker chair by the door. He stared at the floor.

"I've been better," he finally said, his voice low. "What are we going to do?"

"I don't know."

"We have options."

"I know."

There was silence. Melissa watched the snow. She thought about the baby and that word. *Options.* She understood what those options were. None of them appealed to her.

"You can't be pregnant," Matthew said.

"I'm sorry." It was all she could think to say.

"How did this happen?"

"I don't know."

Of course she knew. They both knew. It was a stupid question and a stupid answer.

A few minutes passed.

"I'm sorry," Matthew whispered. His hands were shaking. "Really, I'm sorry."

"Matthew, I love you."

He didn't reply. He stared at the carpet.

"Matthew, I love you," she repeated.

"I love you, too," he said, his voice distant.

"How are we going to tell our parents?"

Matthew watched the floor like a nervous little boy who had done something bad and was waiting for his punishment.

He said, "My father will kill me. And the shit at school. Do you have any idea what they'll say in school?"

Melissa flinched. Last night she had awakened on the floor of her bedroom, drenched in cold sweat from a nightmare. Kids in her biology class had been mocking her, scolding her, asking her if she did it for free or if you had to pay for her services. Her belly was huge in the dream and everyone took turns punching her and she screamed as the front of her dress turned red and the liquefied remains of her baby flowed from between her legs.

So yes, she had concerns about what would be said at school.

"Matthew, we can figure this out."

"We have options. It's really small, right? It doesn't even look like a person."

Melissa didn't reply. She considered what Matthew had said as the ancient alarm clock marked each minute. She was almost hypnotized by how slowly time seemed to be moving and how muddled the thoughts in her brain had become. So little sleep, so many emotions, and yet the Earth just kept spinning and spinning as if she didn't even exist.

Melissa looked out the window again. The snow was falling faster. She thought of her baby. Their baby. The clump of cells like a snowflake. A snowflake growing inside of her. A perfect little snowflake that might land anywhere, do anything.

"I want to keep the baby," Melissa whispered. "We can do this together. I know we can."

For the first time since they left the Diner, Matthew raised his gaze to meet Melissa's hopeful eyes. His hands began to clench and unclench. Faster and faster.

Melissa felt a strange twinge of fear, but something else simmered deep inside her, too. A realization had been nagging at her for most of the night. Right now she didn't actually care what people would say, what people would think. Right now she just wanted Matthew to demonstrate that he loved her as much as he had when he was out of breath, gasping in her ear, promising her the world.

"Do you understand?" Matthew asked as if he had been saying something she didn't hear. He stood and paced back and forth before the window. The snowy world outside was surprisingly bright behind him.

"Understand what?"

Matthew moved faster. Melissa had never seen him agitated like this before. They had known each other since the first grade and she couldn't remember his hands ever shaking this much.

"There's only one way," Matthew said. He removed his father's snub-nosed revolver from the pocket of his baggy pants. The gun was silver with a black grip.

"What are you doing?" Melissa heard the terror in her voice, although she hadn't realized how truly terrified she was until the words escaped her mouth. Her chapped lips burned.

"This is the only way," Matthew said. He stepped forward, extending his right arm.

Once again, Melissa was amazed at how circumstances could change so quickly and so unexpectedly with so little warning. That thought throbbed inside her head, directly behind her eyes, as if a sizzling piece of metal were poking her brain. She wanted to scream. This wasn't the boy she had fallen in love with. He was supposed to love her and support her and give her the world, just as he had promised.

Melissa reached out and her thin fingers grabbed the barrel of the gun, yanking the revolver from Matthew's hand. Surprise flashed in his eyes and he lunged forward, knocking her to the floor. They rolled against the wall and he wrapped one hand around the gun as he pried at her fingers.

They rolled again and suddenly Matthew was on top of her, his weight pushing her against the floor. Their fingers struggled for control of the trigger and then there was a roar of thunder, an unexpected and impossibly loud surge of sound.

A hole appeared in Matthew's hand at the end of the barrel. A matching hole exploded in the middle of his forehead. Blood and gray clumps splashed onto the wall.

Matthew remained frozen, looming above Melissa, his surprised eyes locked on hers. Then he rolled backwards, landing on the threadbare carpet, his eyes still open and staring at the yellowed popcorn ceiling.

The gun fell to the floor with a thud.

Melissa pushed herself away, crawling backwards to the other side of the room. Her heart raced and she didn't think she'd ever be able to slow it down. She couldn't focus on anything except the dead body as her mind screamed, *Get up, get up, get up!* and she didn't know if she meant Matthew or herself.

Time had been moving so fast for a few seconds there, but now it slowed again. The clock on the nightstand ticked away the minutes. Melissa soaked in the heavy silence of the motel room, which was deafening inside her head.

Finally, she stumbled to her feet. The beige walls and her frenzied thoughts spun. She opened the door to the outside. A frigid winter wind blew the falling snow through the doorway. The white flakes landed on the stained carpet.

A chill bit into Melissa. The wind whipped past her thin dress. The pick-up truck's windshield and hood were already white with snow. To her left and right were the other, unoccupied rooms. Dull lights burned along the overhang, creating an eerie chorus line.

Melissa sat on the rocking chair outside the door, the freezing wind biting into her flesh. Snow landed on her skin as the cold attacked her with a savage ferocity. A tear trickled down her face, transforming into a tiny diamond of ice by the time it reached the corner of her mouth.

She rocked and she watched the snow and she clutched her belly tighter. Before too long, the air stopped being so cold and a warmth spread throughout Melissa. The sensation was almost pleasant.

As she rocked, Melissa realized the person she had come here with couldn't have been the real Matthew. Whoever that had been, he acted nothing like the boy she loved so much. He must have been some kind of imposter.

Soon Melissa forgot about the dead body in the motel room and the heart-pounding terror of what had happened.

Instead, she remembered the promises the real Matthew had made her and she waited for him to return while the snow piled higher and higher, forming an ocean of perfect little snowflakes for as far as she could see.

CHADBOURNE

The Plague of Sadness

THE WOMAN DOESN'T REMEMBER WHEN the coldness began to fester inside her, but she's terrified.

Her hand trembles on the doorknob to her baby's nursery. The room is pink and yellow and full of stuffed animals and there are white lacy curtains on the windows. The woman can see the tiniest detail when she closes her eyes, and she tries with all of her might to back away.

There is darkness behind her eyes, but it won't stay still. The darkness moves and dances.

The woman opens the door and steps into the room.

In the corner is the white crib. Anne Marie is asleep, finally asleep, a gift from God that there's sleep after days of crying and fussing and sickness. She looks like a beautiful china doll.

No, no, no, the woman thinks as she reaches for her child. A tear trickles down her face.

Dispatcher (female): 911, what is the nature of your emergency?

Woman's Voice (barely audible): It's *so* cold here.

Dispatcher: Ma'am, you'll have to speak up. What's the nature of your emergency?

Woman's Voice (more clearly): *So cold.*

Dispatcher: Where are you, Ma'am?

Woman's Voice: I just drowned my baby girl.

Dispatcher: What? What happened to your baby?

Woman's Voice: The coldness just won't quit.

(Sound of a gun cocking is clearly audible)

Dispatcher: Ma'am, I'm sending someone to your location, just hold on....

(A gunshot. Then two distinct thumps as the gun and the woman drop to the floor.)
Dispatcher: Oh my God. Ma'am, ma'am? Are you still there? Oh my God, someone get Harry, I think this lady just killed herself!

There is a great deal of paperwork after the call, but Sheila is numb as she provides the required answers. She's never had anyone die on her before. She's certainly had some close calls—the man who cut off his thumb while trying to figure out his new circular saw being a prime example—but nothing like this. Even that Darwin Award runner-up survived. But this woman whose name she doesn't even know because nothing showed up on the call screen hadn't reached out in time, and Sheila had merely been a witness to her death.

Sheila's boss, an older man named Harry Duncan, sits in the tiny break room with her in case she needs anything. He is kind and supportive. No one will blame her for how the call terminated. She responded quickly, she asked the right questions, she hadn't been drinking or sleeping on the job. The call was textbook, even if the outcome wasn't ideal. But the paperwork must be finished, just the same. All of the t's crossed and all of the i's dotted.

Sheila doesn't know whether she'll ever be able to sit at the command console again. She now understands why many dispatchers don't ever come back, not after something like this.

"You did everything you could," Harry tells his shell-shocked employee for the third time as if reading her mind. "I'm not supposed to say this, but some people can't be saved."

Sheila winces. She thinks of her own baby at home, a baby whose father was ripped out of their lives by a drunk driver, the baby who is her last living connection to the man she had loved so completely.

How could you hold your struggling baby in the bathtub until her little face stopped crying and the bubbles ceased to rise from her tiny mouth?

Sheila's mind is spinning with questions and they don't even feel like her own thoughts and she wants to scream. She realizes she *hates* the dead woman. Sheila has never desired to hurt anyone this badly, not even the drunken Steelers fan who killed her husband. Somehow, she even forgave that selfish asshole who didn't even apologize to her in the courtroom. Yet Sheila wishes she could go back in time to yesterday and murder this woman to save the baby and she has no idea how to feel about *that* repeating thought, which just won't quit.

"Why would someone kill her kid?" Sheila is asking herself as much as she is asking Harry or the walls of the room. "How *could* she?"

"I don't know. I just try to bounce back the best I can because there will be more people to help tomorrow."

Sheila signs the last page. Her hands are shaking. "If it's okay, I think I need to leave."

"Do you want a lift?"

"No, I'd rather be alone for a while."

ဖ

Six hours later, Sheila is rocking her sleeping baby in the living room of her pleasant little house on the edge of town. The curtains are pulled nearly shut and the room is dark, but a sliver of moonlight sneaks across the floor.

Outside there are sirens. More sirens than she's ever heard in her life, as if the world is coming to an end. Perhaps it is.

After the disastrous call, Sheila felt so much anger, but eventually that anger sunk deep inside of her, transforming into a coldness that now grips her like a vice.

Sheila doesn't know where the coldness came from yet, but she keeps rocking her baby and she desperately wants to stop thinking about the sound the kettle on the stove makes when the water starts to boil.